SINthetik Messiah

LIES, SECRETS AND DEATH

The following literature was designed to be complimented with music.

You can tune in to the music by accessing the album with the identical title here:

www.sinthetikmessiah.bandcamp.com

All characters and stories within these pages are purely fictional. None of the events depicted are based in reality.

Yet, one cannot dismiss the possibility that this book might serve as a portent for the future — not necessarily for us denizens of Earth, but perhaps for those residing in a galaxy parallel to our own, trillions of light-years away.

Written By Bug Gigabyte

Copyright 2024

Table Of Contents

PROLOGUE
Chapter 1: The Space Race to Colonize

In the year 2060, the discovery of New Terra unfolded against the backdrop of humanity's ever-expanding quest to explore the cosmos. It began with the advent of faster-than-light travel, which allowed humanity to venture beyond the confines of the solar system and embark on journeys to distant stars. After centuries of technological advancement and exploration, humans finally discovered New Terra during an ambitious interstellar mission. Scientists and explorers aboard advanced spacecraft ventured into uncharted regions of space, scanning the cosmos for habitable planets that could sustain human life. Their efforts were rewarded when they stumbled upon New Terra, a lush and fertile world orbiting a distant star. With an atmosphere similar to Earth's and a climate conducive to human habitation.

New Terra appeared to be a promising candidate for colonization. Excited by the discovery, humanity launched further expeditions to study New Terra up close and assess its suitability for settlement. These missions confirmed the planet's potential, revealing vast expanses of fertile land, abundant natural resources, and a hospitable environment capable of supporting human civilization.

As news of the discovery spread, it sparked a wave of excitement and optimism among the people of Earth. For the first time in history, humanity had found a new home among the stars—a beacon of hope in an uncertain universe.

With the necessary infrastructure and technology in place, humanity began the monumental task of colonizing New Terra, establishing settlements and cities across its surface.

The planet soon became a bustling hub of activity, attracting pioneers, settlers, and adventurers of many different types of species from every corner of the galaxy. Despite the challenges and obstacles they faced, humanity persevered, driven by a sense of exploration and a desire to build a better future in this newfound world.

And so, the story of New Terra became intertwined with the epic saga of humanity's journey to the stars; a testament to the indomitable spirit of exploration and discovery that defines us as a species.

New Terra is located in the Orion Arm of the Milky Way Galaxy, relatively close to Earth in cosmic terms. Positioned within a region teeming with star systems and celestial bodies, New Terra occupies a strategic location that has made it a hub of interstellar trade and commerce. Its proximity to other inhabited worlds and key hyperspace routes have contributed to its importance as a center of political and economic activity within the galaxy. Despite its significance, New Terra faces numerous challenges, including overpopulation, resource scarcity and social unrest, all of which shape its complex and dynamic landscape.

By 2200 AD, the living conditions on New Terra
were nothing short of dire. Towering skyscrapers
cast long shadows over crowded streets where
throngs of people shuffled by, their faces etched
with exhaustion and resignation. Overpopulation
was rampant with makeshift shantytowns
sprawling out from the city's center like a
cancerous growth. Families crammed into tiny
apartments, their homes little more than glorified
cubicles stacked atop one another. Basic necessities
such as clean water and nutritious food were in
short supply with many forced to rely on meager
rations provided by the government.
Those who could afford it turned to the black
market where prices were exorbitant and quality
was dubious at best.

Sanitation was practically nonexistent, with
overflowing sewers and piles of garbage lining the
streets. Disease ran rampant through the
overcrowded slums, claiming countless lives each
year. Violence was a constant threat with rival
factions vying for control of what little resources
remained. Gangs roamed the streets, preying on
the weak and vulnerable while the authorities
turned a blind eye in exchange for bribes and
kickbacks. For the vast majority of New Terra's
inhabitants, life was a daily struggle for survival, a
grim existence devoid of hope or opportunity.
And as the gap between the haves and have-nots
widened, resentment simmered beneath the
surface, threatening to boil over into open revolt at
any moment.

Chapter 2: Rise from the Ashes

In the sprawling metropolis of New Terra, amidst the neon glow of skyscrapers and the hum of hovercraft, lived a man named Alden Vance. Born into poverty in the lower levels of the city, Alden sought out a living as a mechanic, repairing outdated starships to make ends meet. His workshop, nestled in the shadows of towering buildings, echoed with the clang of metal against metal, a testament to his tireless work ethic.

Alden's life changed forever during the Battle of New Terra in 2190 AD, a brutal conflict between rival alien races vying for control of the planet's rich resources. The chaos of war descended upon the city like a storm, tearing apart families and leaving destruction in its wake.

Amidst the rubble and smoke, Alden emerged as a beacon of hope, displaying remarkable courage and cunning as he darted between crumbling buildings to rescue civilians trapped in the crossfire. His heart pounded with adrenaline as he dodged enemy fire, his mind racing with strategies to outmaneuver the invaders. Impressed by his actions, General Solan, the grizzled commander of the planetary defense force, offered Alden a position in the military.

With nothing to lose and everything to gain, Alden accepted, leaving behind his old life in pursuit of a new destiny. He traded his greasy overalls for the crisp uniform of a soldier, his determination burning bright as he embarked on his journey into the unknown.

As Alden trained with the other recruits, he proved himself to be a natural leader, earning the respect and admiration of his peers. His unwavering dedication and sharp mind set him apart from the others, catching the eye of his superiors. Despite his humble beginnings, Alden quickly rose through the ranks, his skills in combat and strategic thinking propelling him forward. Days turned into weeks, weeks into months, and months into years.

Alden's rise through the military ranks was swift and decisive. His leadership on the battlefield was unmatched, his strategic brilliance turning the tide of countless skirmishes. With each victory, his legend grew, and his name was whispered in awe by both friend and foe alike. But amidst the accolades and praise, Alden remained grounded, never forgetting his humble origins. He never lost sight of the people he had sworn to protect, the civilians whose lives hung in the balance with each passing day. Their faces haunted his dreams and their suffering had become etched into his soul like a scar that would never fade.

As Alden's reputation soared, so too did the expectations that were now placed upon him. The weight of leadership bore down upon his shoulders like a heavy burden. Filling his mind with breadth and gravity. But Alden faced each challenge with unwavering resolve, his determination unyielding in the face of adversity.

And so, as the years passed and Alden's influence continued to grow, he found himself at the forefront of a new era in New Terra's history. The once war-torn city began to rebuild, its scars slowly fading beneath the glow of newfound prosperity. And at the center of it all stood Alden Vance, a beacon of hope in a galaxy consumed by darkness.

Chapter 3: His Descent Into Darkness

As Alden continued to ascend within the military hierarchy, his ambitions grew ever larger. He began to see himself not just as a soldier, but as a leader destined for greatness. The whispers of power and prestige seduced him, fueling a hunger that gnawed at his soul. With each promotion came a deeper descent into darkness. Alden's thirst for power blinded him to the consequences of his actions, and he began to manipulate and deceive those around him to further his own agenda.

He traded honesty for manipulation, sacrificing his integrity in the pursuit of his ambitions. As the stress mounted, Alden turned to drugs as a means of escape, seeking solace in the oblivion they promised. What started as occasional indulgence soon spiraled into full-blown addiction, consuming him like a ravenous beast. Under the influence of narcotics, Alden's judgment became clouded, his actions erratic and unpredictable. He surrounded himself with sycophants and enablers who fueled his descent into darkness with their own agendas and desires.

In the grip of his addiction, Alden's once noble ideals were twisted beyond recognition, replaced by a hunger for power and control. He lashed out at those who dared to oppose him, resorting to violence and intimidation to maintain his grip on power.

As rumors of Alden's depravity spread, dissent simmered beneath the surface of New Terra, threatening to erupt into open rebellion. But Alden's iron grip on the planet remained unyielding. His hold on power is seemingly unshakable. The streets of New Terra ran red with blood as Alden's reign of terror reached its zenith, leaving a scar on the planet that would never fully heal. And though he would eventually emerge from the depths of his addiction, the damage had already been done, and the stain of his crimes would haunt New Terra for generations to come.

Chapter 4: Redemption and Sacrifice

As Alden's reign of terror stretched into its third decade, a spark of conscience flickered within his heart. Haunted by the ghosts of his past and the suffering he had caused, Alden began to question the morality of his actions. He saw the suffering etched into the faces of his people and felt the weight of their oppression pressing down upon him like a suffocating blanket.

In the year 2225, the war with the mechanoids was a pivotal moment in Alden Vance's reign as Supreme Commander of New Terra. It began with the discovery of a previously unknown mechanoid civilization on the outskirts of the galaxy, a race of sentient machines whose technology far surpassed anything humanity had ever encountered.

At first, Alden saw the mechanoids as a potential threat to New Terra's dominance in the galaxy. He ordered a series of reconnaissance missions to gather intelligence on their capabilities and intentions, hoping to assess the level of danger they posed. However, as the true extent of the mechanoids' power became clear, Alden's apprehension turned to fear.

The mechanoids were unlike anything humanity had ever faced before — cold, calculating, and utterly devoid of mercy. Faced with the prospect of an all-out war with an enemy of unparalleled strength, Alden made the fateful decision to strike first.

He mobilized New Terra's vast military machine, marshaling its resources for a preemptive strike against the mechanoids' fleet of spaceships. The ensuing conflict was brutal and devastating with both sides suffering heavy casualties. The mechanoids, though outnumbered, possessed technology far superior to anything humanity had at its disposal, and their war machines cut through Alden's forces with ruthless efficiency. Despite the overwhelming odds against them, Alden and his troops fought valiantly, determined to protect New Terra at any cost. But as the war dragged on, it became increasingly clear that victory was slipping from their grasp.

In a last-ditch effort to turn the tide of battle, Alden authorized the use of experimental weapons developed in secret by New Terra's top scientists who worked for the Religious Council. These devastating devices unleashed untold destruction upon the mechanoid forces, but at a terrible cost—death.

As the final showdown loomed on the horizon, Alden knew that the fate of New Terra hung in the balance. With the weight of the galaxy bearing down upon him, he faced his greatest challenge yet, confronting the demons of his past and the uncertainty of the future. But even as the odds stacked against him, Alden refused to back down, determined to see his mission through to the bitter end.

So, in a climactic battle that shook the very foundations of the galaxy, Alden made the ultimate sacrifice. With his dying breath, he unleashed a wave of energy that crippled the enemy into submission.

In the end, the war with the mechanoids left the galaxy scarred and battered, its once-mighty military humbled by defeat. Alden Vance, once hailed as a hero, was forced to reckon with the consequences of his actions as the galaxy watched in horror at the devastation wrought by his ambition and hubris.

Though Alden's name would be forever remembered as that of a dictator and tyrant, his legacy endured as a beacon of hope that humans will always control this galaxy.

Despite Alden Vance's demise, his followers showed no signs of relenting in their pursuit of power and control. In fact, his death seemed to embolden them, strengthening their resolve to maintain their grip on the galaxy at all costs.

In secrecy, his inner circle scrambled to fill the power vacuum left in his wake. They vied for dominance. Each member sought to assert their authority and secure their position within the hierarchy of the galactic empire. Each one vying for supremacy and willing to resort to any means necessary to achieve their goals. Murder was just one of the means.

Under the guise of maintaining order and stability, Alden's followers tightened their control over the galaxy, imposing harsher restrictions and more oppressive measures upon its inhabitants. Dissent was swiftly crushed, dissenters silenced or eliminated without mercy. Meanwhile, whispers of corruption and tyranny spread like wildfire throughout the galaxy.

Despite the risks, pockets of rebellion began to emerge, fueled by a fierce determination to overthrow the oppressive regime and restore freedom to the galaxy. But the Empire's hold on power remained firm, bolstered by its vast resources and formidable military machine.

Those who dared to oppose it faced insurmountable odds, their struggles often ending in tragedy and defeat.

As the galaxy plunged deeper into darkness, hope seemed like a distant memory, a flickering flame struggling to survive amidst the encroaching shadows. Though Alden Vance may have fallen, his legacy lived on in the form of the Empire he had helped to create—a dark and oppressive force that threatened to consume everything in its path.

WHEN THE WORLD IS ON FIRE

Chapter 1: When The Cities Burn

Under the new regime, New Terra plunged into a state of lawlessness and despair. Alden's former enforcers, emboldened by their newfound authority, ruled with an iron fist, quashing any semblance of dissent with ruthless efficiency. Those who dared to speak out against the regime faced swift and brutal reprisals.

With Alden's absence, the delicate balance that had kept the city's infrastructure functioning began to unravel. Basic services crumbled under the weight of neglect and corruption. Clean water became scarce, food supplies dwindled, and medical care became a luxury reserved for the privileged few. Poverty and desperation spread like wildfire through the planet, as once-prosperous neighborhoods decayed into slums teeming with crime and despair. Homelessness soared as families were displaced from their homes, forced to seek out a meager existence in the shadows of towering skyscrapers.

Meanwhile, Alden's loyalists lined their pockets with ill-gotten gains, siphoning off the planet's resources for their own selfish ends. Corruption ran rampant with bribery and extortion becoming the norm as those in power sought to enrich themselves at the expense of the suffering masses.

Amidst the chaos and despair, whispers of rebellion began to stir once more. But any attempts to challenge the oppressive regime were swiftly crushed by Alden's former enforcers, who showed no mercy to those who dared to defy their authority. As the weeks turned into months, and the months into years, the situation on New Terra grew increasingly dire. The once-vibrant cityscape became a wasteland of broken dreams and shattered hopes, its people trapped in a cycle of violence and despair with no end in sight.

Chapter 2: The Voice of Truth

In the sprawling metropolis of New Terra, the Galactic Tribune headquarters rose like a beacon of transparency against the night sky. Its imposing facade hinted at the stories within, its secrets waiting to be unearthed by intrepid journalists and truth-seekers alike.

Within the conference room of the Tribune, anticipation hung thick in the air like a tangible presence. Journalists from every corner of the galaxy had converged, eager to witness history unfold before their very eyes. At the center of it all stood Marcus Reynolds, a figure of quiet resolve amidst the bustling crowd. Clad in a simple suit that belied the weight of the truths he carried, he exuded an air of determination.

As Marcus took his place behind the podium, the room fell silent, every eye trained on him expectantly. Before speaking in a voice that carried the weight of the galaxy's expectations.
He cleared his throat, the sound echoed off the walls like a gunshot.

"Ladies and gentlemen of the press," Marcus began, his words measured and deliberate.

"Today, I stand before you not merely as a whistleblower, but as a guardian of truth—a truth that has been shrouded in darkness for far too long."

The room hung on his every word as Marcus recounted the journey that had led him to this pivotal moment—the years spent in service to the late Supreme Commander Alden Vance, the horrors witnessed, the injustices uncovered. His narrative wove a tapestry of betrayal and deceit, painting a picture of a regime built on the suffering of the innocent.

As images flickered across the screen behind him—footage of clandestine meetings, reports of mass surveillance, testimonials from survivors of Alden Vance's brutal reign—the gravity of Marcus's allegations became impossible to ignore. The once untouchable legacy of the late Supreme Commander crumbled before the eyes of the galaxy exposing the rot at its core.

"We cannot allow the sins of the past to go unpunished," Marcus declared, his voice ringing with righteous fury.

"It is our duty, as seekers of truth, to hold those responsible to account for their crimes. For the sake of justice, for the memory of the countless lives lost, we must ensure that Alden Vance's legacy is one of condemnation, not adulation."

The journalists erupted into a frenzy of questions, their voices blending together in a cacophony of curiosity and disbelief. Marcus fielded them with grace and composure, each response a testament to his unwavering commitment to the pursuit of justice.

But amidst the chaos of the press conference, one question lingered like a specter in the room—a question that struck at the heart of Marcus's motivations, the driving force behind his decision to come forward now after so many years of silence.

"Why now?" a young reporter's voice tinged with skepticism.

"Why choose to speak out against Alden Vance's regime only after his death?" Marcus met her gaze, his expression unyielding.

"Because the truth cannot be buried forever," he replied.

"And justice delayed is justice denied. I may have once served under Alden Vance but I refuse to be complicit in his crimes. It is my duty, as a citizen of the galaxy, to shine a light on the darkness that has festered for far too long."

With that, Marcus stepped away from the podium. As he made his way through the throng of reporters, he felt a sense of relief wash over him—a burden lifted, replaced by the knowledge that he had done his part to expose the truth and bring about change.

As he made his way through the throng of reporters and onlookers, a figure closed in, blending seamlessly into the crowd. Suddenly, with a deafening roar, an explosion ripped through the air, sending shockwaves of chaos and panic cascading through the crowd. In the chaos that followed, Marcus and several innocent news reporters were caught in the blast.

The once defiant voice of truth was silenced in an instant, his courageous stand against tyranny cut tragically short. The news of Marcus's death sent shockwaves throughout the galaxy, a grim reminder of the dangers that awaited those who dared to challenge the status quo. But even in death, Marcus's legacy lived on.

As the smoke cleared and the dust settled, the galaxy mourned the loss of one of its bravest voices. But amidst the grief and sorrow, a steely resolve took hold—a determination to honor Marcus's memory by continuing the struggle against oppression and tyranny no matter the cost.

Chapter 3: True Intentions

In the wake of the bombing, the galaxy erupted into speculation and chaos.

The attack had been meticulously orchestrated to cast suspicion on Alden Vance's regime making it appear as though they were attempting to silence Marcus and send a chilling message to anyone who dared to challenge their authority.

The recently defeated mechanoids had played their hand masterfully, exploiting the tensions and fears that had gripped the galaxy in the aftermath of Alden's death. With Marcus's demise, they had effectively started to sow seeds of doubt and mistrust among the populace.

Whispers of conspiracy began to spread like wildfire. Some believed that Alden's regime was indeed behind the attack, seeking to silence Marcus and quash any dissent against their rule. Others suspected a darker force at play, a force that lurked in the shadows and manipulated events from behind the scenes. The Religious Council.

As investigations into the bombing unfolded, the truth remained elusive, obscured by layers of deception and intrigue. The mechanoids watched from the shadows, their sinister agenda inching ever closer to fruition with each passing day.

Meanwhile, Marcus's death sent shockwaves through the galaxy, igniting a firestorm of outrage and indignation. His legacy as a champion of truth and justice endured, even in death, inspiring others to take up his mantle and continue the fight against corruption and tyranny.

But as the galaxy plunged deeper into darkness, the mechanoids watched with satisfaction knowing that their plans were proceeding according to schedule. With Marcus out of the way and suspicion cast upon Alden's regime, they were one step closer to achieving their ultimate goal of revenge against humanity.

Chapter 4: Uprising

A group of like-minded individuals emerged from the shadows united by a common desire for justice and revenge. Disillusioned by the ineffectiveness of traditional channels and outraged by the brazen act of violence that had silenced Marcus's voice, they took matters into their own hands.

Gathering in secret meeting places across the galaxy, these individuals swore oaths of loyalty to their fallen comrade and vowed to carry on his fight against tyranny. They came from all walks of life — former soldiers, activists, ordinary citizens driven to action by the injustice they witnessed.

United by their shared grief and righteous anger, they formed their own militia, training tirelessly in the art of combat and guerrilla warfare. They honed their skills in the shadows, preparing for the day when they would exact their revenge upon those responsible for the death of so many.

Armed with determination and a burning desire for justice, they launched covert operations against Alden Vance's loyalists, striking with precision and anonymity. They sabotaged supply lines, disrupted communications networks, and targeted key figures within the regime, striking fear into the hearts of their oppressors. But their ultimate goal remained elusive — to bring Alden Vance's loyalists to justice and avenge Marcus Reynolds' untimely death.

With each passing day, their resolve only grew stronger, fueled by the memory of their fallen comrade and the belief that no act of tyranny should go unpunished. As they waged their clandestine war against Alden Vance's regime, they became symbols of resistance and defiance while inspiring others to join their cause. Their ranks swelled with each new recruit, each one drawn to the promise of a better future and the hope of one day seeing justice served.

THE LOST COGNITIVE FIGHT
Chapter 1: A Public Figure Arises

One year after Alden Vance's reign, his galactic empire grew stronger. At the heart of this turmoil stood a young and idealistic leader, Ezra Halcyon, whose unwavering resolve and boundless courage inspired hope in the hearts of countless beings across the stars. He had witnessed first-hand the atrocities committed under Alden Vance's rule.

Determined to bring about change, Ezra rallied a disparate coalition of rebels, outcasts, and freedom fighters united in their quest to overthrow the tyrannical remnants of the growing galactic empire.

Together, they embarked on a daring campaign to liberate oppressed worlds and dismantle the machinery of oppression that had kept the galaxy in chains for far too long. But the road to freedom was fraught with peril as the forces of darkness marshaled their strength to crush the burgeoning rebellion before it could gain momentum.

Led by ruthless warlords and cunning tacticians, they sought to maintain their grip on power at any cost. They unleashed their formidable fleets and legions of mech suited soldiers to crush dissent wherever it arose.

Amidst the chaos of war, Ezra's resolve was tested like never before, as he grappled with the weight of leadership and the sacrifices demanded by the struggle for freedom. He faced betrayal and treachery from within his own ranks as ambitious rivals sought to seize control for themselves and undermine his authority at every turn.

As the conflict raged on, Ezra and his allies scored victories against the empire, striking blows against its forces and inspiring hope in the hearts of countless beings across the galaxy. It was a fight not just for survival, but for the very soul of the galaxy itself—a battle between light and darkness, hope and despair.

Chapter 2: Revelation

Five years later, Ezra stood amidst the rubble of a once-thriving city, the echoes of war ringing in his ears like a cacophony of despair. The smoke-filled sky cast a pall over the landscape, obscuring the sun and suffocating the hope that had once burned bright in his heart. As he surveyed the devastation around him, Ezra felt a profound sense of disillusionment wash over him—a realization that shook him to his core.

For years, he had fought and bled in the name of a cause he believed to be just—a cause that had promised freedom, justice, and prosperity for all. But now, as he gazed upon the destruction wrought by war, he could no longer ignore the harsh truth that lay before him.

In that moment of clarity, Ezra experienced a profound epiphany—a revelation that cut through the fog of confusion and uncertainty that had clouded his mind for so long. He realized that the cycle of violence and bloodshed could never lead to true peace. Rather, the path he had chosen had only brought pain and suffering to those he sought to protect.

With a heavy heart, Ezra dropped to his knees. Tears welled in his eyes as he reflected on the lives lost, the families torn apart, and the dreams shattered by the ravages of war. He thought of all those who had sacrificed everything in the name of a cause they believed in—a cause that had ultimately led to their demise.

In that moment of vulnerability, Ezra found the strength to acknowledge his own culpability — to accept responsibility for the role he had played in perpetuating the cycle of violence that had consumed his world. He realized that he could no longer continue down the path of destruction, blinded by the false promises of glory and honor. He knew that he had to make a stand — a stand for peace, for reconciliation and for the future of humanity.

Rising to his feet, Ezra made a solemn vow — a vow to lay down his arms and seek a different path — a path of forgiveness, compassion, and understanding. He knew that the road ahead would be long and arduous, fraught with challenges and obstacles. But he also knew that it was a journey worth undertaking — a journey toward a brighter tomorrow, where swords would be beaten into plowshares and the cries of war would be silenced forever.
With newfound determination burning in his heart, Ezra set out to spread his message of peace — to inspire others to join him in his quest to build a world free from the scourge of war. For he knew that true victory could only be achieved through unity, cooperation, and the unwavering belief in the inherent goodness of humanity.

Chapter 3: Ezra's Message

War.

It is a word that weighs heavily on the hearts of all who hear it—a word that conjures images of destruction, suffering, and loss. Yet, despite its horrors, war remains a stubborn fixture of our collective history—a relentless specter that haunts our past, present, and future.

But why? Why do we continue to wage war, knowing full well the devastation it brings?

Is it greed, ambition, or the lust for power?

Is it fear, insecurity, or the need for self-preservation?

Or is it simply the inevitability of human nature—a dark reflection of our inherent flaws and shortcomings?

Regardless of the reasons, one thing remains clear: war is not the answer. It is not a solution to our problems, nor is it a path to lasting peace and prosperity.

War only begets more war, perpetuating a cycle of violence and suffering that knows no end.

Consider the toll that war exacts on our societies—the lives lost, the families torn apart, the communities shattered. Think of the trillions spent on weapons of destruction—resources that could have been invested in education, healthcare, and infrastructure.

Contemplate the environmental devastation wrought by war—the scorched earth, the polluted air, the poisoned waters.

And yet, despite all this, war persists. It persists because we allow it to—because we fail to recognize the futility of violence as a means of resolving our differences. It persists because we cling to the misguided belief that might makes right—that the strong have the authority to dictate the fate of the weak.

But I say to you today: enough is enough. It is time for us to break free from the chains of war and embrace a new paradigm—a paradigm of peace, cooperation, and mutual respect. It is time for us to put aside our differences and work together to build a better future for ourselves and for generations to come.

Let us not be swayed by the false promises of glory and conquest. Let us not be blinded by the allure of power and dominion.

Instead, let us strive for understanding, empathy, and dialogue. Let us seek common ground, build bridges, and forge alliances based on mutual trust and cooperation. In the words of Earth's President John F. Kennedy, "Mankind must put an end to war, or war will put an end to mankind."

These words ring as true today as they did when they were first spoken.
The choice is ours to make.

Will we continue down the path of destruction, or will we chart a new course—a course of peace, prosperity, and progress?

The answer lies within each and every one of us.

Let us choose wisely, for the future of our world depends on it.

Chapter 4: The Pen Is Mightier Than the Sword

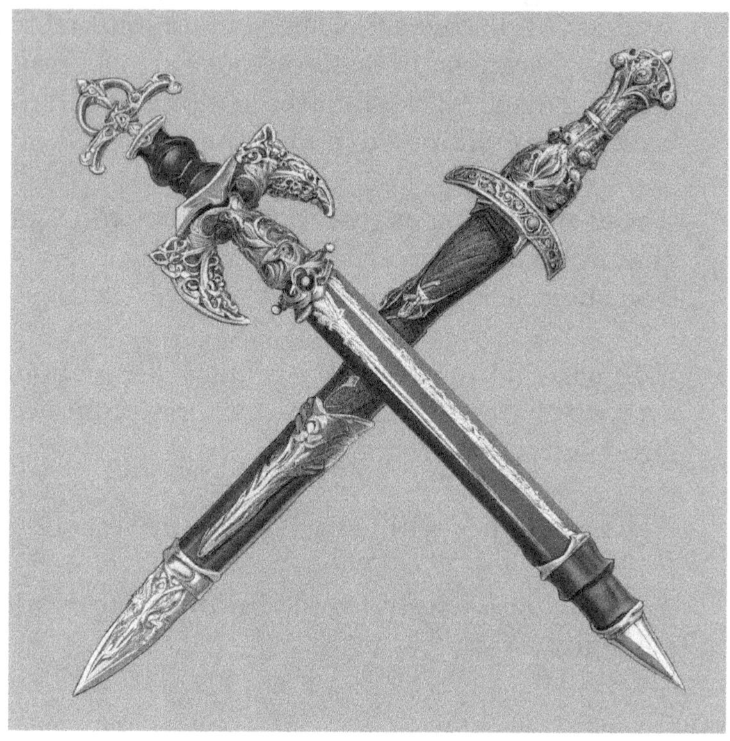

Ezra, having experienced the brutality of war firsthand, understood the power of words to shape minds and hearts in ways that violence never could. He believed that the pen was mightier than the sword because of its ability to influence and inspire change on a deeper level.

To Ezra, the sword represented brute force and coercion, a tool used to subjugate and dominate through fear and intimidation. While it could certainly achieve immediate results, its impact was often fleeting and shallow.

Violence, he knew, could silence dissent in the short term, but it could never truly quell the seeds of rebellion that lay dormant within the human spirit.

On the other hand, the pen symbolized the power of ideas and ideals, the ability to sway hearts and minds through reasoned argument and impassioned rhetoric.

Words, Ezra believed, had the power to transcend barriers and unite people across vast distances and disparate cultures. They could inspire empathy, foster understanding, and ignite movements that could change the course of history. Moreover, Ezra recognized that the written word possessed a permanence that violence could never match.

While the effects of a sword strike might fade with time, the impact of a well-crafted argument or a stirring speech could endure for generations. It can shape the thoughts and actions of countless individuals long after the ink has dried.

In essence, Ezra saw the pen as a weapon of peace, a tool that could be wielded to break down walls and build bridges, to illuminate the darkness and bring about lasting change. While the sword may win battles, he believed, it was ultimately the power of words that would win the war for the soul of humanity.

Ezra's message of peace and reconciliation spread far and wide throughout the galaxy thanks in large part to his prolific writing and savvy media presence.

As an accomplished author, he penned numerous books and treatises that explored themes of empathy, cooperation, and understanding. These works resonated with readers from all walks of life, inspiring them to rethink their assumptions and embrace a more inclusive worldview.

Through his books, Ezra reached audiences on distant planets and remote colonies, offering them a glimpse into his vision for a better, more harmonious future.

His writings were translated into thousands of languages and distributed across the galaxy, becoming required reading in schools, universities, and community centers alike. From the bustling metropolises of core worlds to the frontier outposts on the galactic fringe, Ezra's words found eager ears and receptive hearts.

But it wasn't just his books that spread Ezra's message — it was also his skillful use of the media.

Recognizing the power of mass communication, he made regular appearances on talk shows, podcasts, and news programs across the galaxy. Through interviews and panel discussions, he engaged directly with audiences, answering their questions and addressing their concerns with wisdom and compassion.

Through live streams and interactive forums, he engaged with viewers in real time, fostering a sense of connection and community that transcended physical distance. Moreover, Ezra's influence extended beyond the realm of print and broadcast media. He also leveraged social networks and galactic online platforms to amplify his message and mobilize supporters.

Through blogs, forums, and social media profiles, he cultivated a global network of like-minded individuals who shared his commitment to peace and social justice. In this way, Ezra's message became a beacon of hope for countless beings across the galaxy, offering them a guiding light in an uncertain universe.

Through the power of his words and the reach of modern media, he sparked a movement that would shape the course of history for generations to come.

I'M ON FIRE

Chapter 1: Alden's Legacy: The Flames of Destruction

In a galaxy torn asunder by the relentless pursuit of power, two factions stood on the precipice of annihilation, each vying for dominance in the wake of Alden Vance's reign of terror. The air crackled with tension as nuclear weapons loomed ominously overhead.

On one side of the conflict stood the Vanguard of Freedom, a coalition of rebel forces united in their defiance against Alden's tyranny. Led by General Elena Rivera, a fearless commander with an unshakable resolve, the Vanguard had sworn to liberate the galaxy from the grip of oppression, no matter the cost.

Opposing them were the Remnants of Alden's empire, a fanatical regime hell-bent on preserving the legacy of their fallen leader at any cost. Under the command of Chancellor Markus Reinhardt, another ruthless dictator with a thirst for power, the Remnants sought to crush all who dared to challenge their authority with an iron fist.

As the conflict escalated, tensions reached a boiling point and both sides found themselves hurtling towards the brink of oblivion.

With each passing day, the threat of nuclear annihilation loomed ever larger, casting a dark shadow over the galaxy and plunging it into chaos and despair.

In the heart of the Vanguard's command center, Elena stood resolute as she surveyed the grim reality of the war-torn galaxy. The once-great civilizations lay in ruins. Yet amidst the devastation, a glimmer of hope still burned bright in the general's heart, a beacon of defiance against the darkness that threatened to consume them all.

Across the battlefield, Chancellor Reinhardt gazed out from the towering spires of his fortress. His eyes ablaze with a fanatical zeal that brooked no dissent.

To him, victory was not just an option—it was a necessity, a validation of Alden's twisted vision for the galaxy and the culmination of years of ruthless ambition.

The battlefield was a desolate wasteland, littered with the debris of war and soaked with the blood of fallen soldiers. Dark clouds loomed overhead, casting ominous shadows across the scorched earth below. Amidst the chaos stood two figures of power locked in a deadly dance of destruction.

Chapter 2: The Battlefield

The battlefield stretched out before them like a vast expanse of desolation, scarred by the ravages of war and littered with the detritus of battle. The air was thick with the acrid scent of smoke and burning metal, mingling with the stench of death and decay. Dark clouds hung low in the sky, casting ominous shadows across the landscape below.

On one side of the battlefield stood the forces of Chancellor Reinhardt, their ranks arrayed in disciplined formations, their weapons gleaming in the dim light. They marched forward with grim determination, their footsteps echoing across the barren wasteland as they advanced towards their enemy.

Opposing them were the soldiers of Elena's resistance movement, a ragtag band of rebels united by a common cause. They fought with a fierce determination born of desperation. Their weapons held aloft as they prepared to meet their foe head-on.

The landscape itself was a study in contrasts with jagged mountains looming in the distance and vast plains stretching out as far as the eye could see. Rivers of molten lava snaked their way across the battlefield, casting an eerie glow upon the twisted landscape.

Amidst the chaos of battle, mechanized suits of armor lumbered forward, their massive frames towering over the battlefield like ancient colossi.

These formidable war machines were the backbone of Reinhardt's army. Their armored plating bristling with weapons and their mechanical limbs capable of crushing steel and bone alike. But for all their might, the mechanized suits were not invincible. Many had been damaged in previous battles. Their once-imposing forms reduced to little more than twisted wrecks of metal and circuitry. Yet still they pressed forward. Their pilots undeterred by the grim specter of death that loomed over them.

As the two armies clashed, the battlefield erupted into chaos, with explosions rocking the earth and gunfire echoing through the air. The mechanized suits unleashed a barrage of missiles and laser fire, cutting through the ranks of Elena's forces with ruthless efficiency.

But the rebels fought on despite the overwhelming odds stacked against them. They moved with a fluidity born of desperation, darting between cover and trading blows with their heavily armored adversaries.

In the midst of the carnage, Elena stood tall inside her mech suit. Her sword held aloft as she led her troops into battle. Her eyes burned with a fierce determination. Her every movement is a testament to her unwavering commitment to the cause.

As the battle raged on, the landscape became a nightmarish tableau of destruction and death. Bodies littered the ground, their lifeless forms a grim reminder of the cost of war. Yet still the fighting continued, each side locked in a desperate struggle for survival.

But amidst the chaos and bloodshed, a flicker of hope remained — a spark of defiance that refused to be extinguished. For as long as there were those willing to stand up and fight, there would always be hope for a brighter tomorrow, even in the darkest of times.

Chapter 3: The Losing Battle

Elena, her eyes ablaze with determination, faced off against Chancellor Reinhardt, the embodiment of tyranny and oppression. Their swords clashed with a deafening clang sending sparks flying into the air like fiery embers. Each blow reverberated through the air with bone-shaking force, a testament to the sheer power and ferocity of their mechanized suits. As they fought, the ground trembled beneath their feet, unable to withstand the sheer force of their clashes. Craters formed in their wake, swallowing whole swathes of the battlefield in a maelstrom of destruction. The air was thick with the acrid scent of smoke and sweat, mingling with the coppery tang of blood.

Elena's movements were swift and fluid, her sword dancing through the air with deadly precision. She ducked and weaved, dodging Reinhardt's strikes with practiced ease before launching a counterattack of her own. With each swing of her blade, she carved through the air like a whirlwind of death, her eyes never leaving her opponent's.

Reinhardt, however, was a formidable adversary, his strength and resolve matched only by his ruthless cunning. He fought with the ferocity of a cornered beast. His every move is calculated to inflict maximum damage upon his foe. His eyes burned with an unholy fire, devoid of mercy or compassion.

As the battle raged on, the two combatants pushed themselves to their limits. Their mech suits battered and bruised, but their spirits unbroken. They fought not just for victory, but for something far greater—for the fate of the galaxy hung in the balance, teetering on the brink of oblivion. But amidst the chaos and carnage, a sense of unease began to creep into Elena's mind—a nagging doubt that whispered of darker truths lurking beneath the surface.

She saw glimpses of Reinhardt's true nature, the depths of his depravity laid bare for all to see. His eyes held a madness that chilled her to the bone, a hunger for power that knew no bounds. With a sinking feeling in her heart, Elena realized the true extent of the evil she faced—a darkness that threatened to consume everything in its path. And as she squared off against Reinhardt once more, she knew that this battle would not end until one of them lay broken and defeated upon the blood-soaked ground.

In a final, desperate bid for victory, Elena unleashed a flurry of attacks. Her sword was a blur of motion as she sought to overwhelm her opponent.

But Reinhardt was ready, his defenses impenetrable,and his resolve unyielding. With a savage roar, he launched a devastating counterattack. His sword slicing through the air with lethal precision.

Elena's world exploded into pain as Reinhardt's blade found its mark, clearing through her armor and severing her real arm clean off. She cried out in agony. In that moment of despair, she knew that she had been outmatched—that her quest for justice had come to a bitter and tragic end.

As darkness closed in around her, Elena felt a sense of profound sadness wash over her—a sense of failure that weighed heavy on her soul. She had fought with every ounce of her being, but in the end, it had not been enough.

And as she was slipping into unconsciousness, she prayed that her sacrifice would not be in vain—that others would rise up to take her place and continue the fight against tyranny and oppression.

"In the name of freedom," Elena whispered, staying true to her own convictions.

As the battle reached its climax, Elena found herself cornered, her forces decimated and her options dwindling. With no hope of victory and her enemies closing in, she made a desperate decision.

Activating the self-destruct mechanism within her mobile suit, she unleashed a catastrophic explosion that engulfed the battlefield in a blinding flash of light. The shockwave rippled across the landscape, flattening everything in its path and reducing the once-proud armies to little more than ash and rubble. The force of the blast was felt for miles around, shaking the very foundations of the earth and shattering the tranquility of the surrounding landscape.

Chancellor Reinhardt stood defiant, his own mobile suit braced against the fury of the explosion. But even his formidable armor could not withstand the full force of the blast. As the flames consumed him, his defiant expression melted away into one of shock and horror.

In that moment, the battlefield was transformed into a scene of unimaginable destruction, with twisted wreckage and scorched earth stretching out as far as the eye could see.

Silence laid upon the land.

The once-great armies lay broken and defeated, their hopes of victory crushed beneath the weight of their own arrogance.

DON'T LOSE WHO YOU ARE

Chapter 1: My Brother

In the wake of Alden's sacrifice, his right-hand man, Victor, found himself adrift in a sea of chaos and uncertainty.

For years, he had stood by Alden's side, loyal to the end. His every action guided by the will of his leader. But now, with Alden gone, Victor was left to navigate the treacherous waters of the galactic empire alone.

As he grappled with the loss of his mentor and friend, Victor felt a profound sense of emptiness settle over him—a void that seemed impossible to fill. Memories of their time together haunted him, the weight of their shared experiences bearing down on his weary soul.

But amidst the grief and despair, a flicker of anger smoldered within Victor's heart—a burning ember of resentment that threatened to consume him from within. For though he had served Alden faithfully, he could not shake the feeling that he had been betrayed, cast aside like a pawn in a game of cosmic proportions.

Desperate to cling to his sanity, Victor threw himself into his work with a renewed sense of purpose, determined to honor Alden's memory by preserving the legacy they had built together. But with each passing day, the burden of leadership grew heavier, the weight of responsibility crushing him beneath its unrelenting gaze.

Haunted by visions of Alden's final moments, Victor found himself plagued by doubt and uncertainty, his mind a battlefield of conflicting emotions.

Had Alden truly believed in the righteousness of his sacrifice, or had he been driven to desperation by forces beyond his control?

As Victor grappled with these questions, he found solace in the memories of their shared triumphs—the battles won, the enemies vanquished, the lives saved. But even as he sought refuge in the past, he could not escape the harsh reality of the present—a reality in which the galactic empire stood on the brink of era, its future uncertain.

With the weight of the galaxy bearing down upon him, Victor knew that he could not afford to falter, not now, not ever.

He had sworn an oath to uphold Alden's vision, to safeguard the empire from those who sought to destroy it from within.

And though the road ahead was fraught with peril, he would not rest until his mission was complete.

Chapter 2: Observations of War

Victor stood atop a distant mountain peak, overlooking the battlefield. His eyes fixed on the chaos unfolding below.

From his elevated perch, Victor observed the battlefield below with a keen eye, seeing not just chaos, but an intricate dance of life and death playing out before him.

The movements of the soldiers and their mechanized suits resembled a carefully choreographed performance. Clashing in fierce combat, their movements seemed almost rhythmic, like dancers moving to an unseen beat.Each step was calculated and deliberate.

The ebb and flow of battle created a mesmerizing spectacle, drawing Victor's gaze as he took in the fluidity of the fight.

The landscape itself became a stage for this deadly dance, its rugged terrain serving as both obstacle and advantage for those engaged in combat.

Soldiers ducked behind rocky outcrops for cover. Their movements blended seamlessly with the natural contours of the land.

In the distance, explosions lit up the sky like fireworks, casting an eerie glow over the battlefield.

The air was thick with the smell of smoke and ozone. The sounds of gunfire and explosions reverberated through the air like a symphony of destruction.

Despite the chaos and violence, there was a strange beauty to the scene unfolding before Victor's eyes.

It was a reminder of the resilience of the human spirit, the indomitable will to fight against all odds. But amidst the beauty, there was also tragedy.

Lives were being lost with each passing moment, sacrifices made in the name of ideology and power. As Victor watched the battle unfold. He couldn't help but feel a sense of admiration for the skill and determination of his adversaries.

Elena, with her fierce determination and unwavering resolve, fought with a ferocity that commanded respect. Despite knowing she was fighting for the opposing side, Victor couldn't help but admire her courage and tenacity.

Chancellor Reinhardt, on the other hand, was a different story. While Victor couldn't deny the man's skill and prowess on the battlefield, there was something about his arrogance that rubbed him the wrong way. Reinhardt fought with a sense of entitlement, as if victory were already assured simply because he fought for Alden's cause.

But for all his arrogance, Victor couldn't deny that Reinhardt was a formidable opponent. His devotion to Alden's cause was unwavering, his loyalty to his leader absolute. It was this dedication that made him both a dangerous enemy and a worthy adversary.

As the battle raged on, Victor found himself torn between his admiration for Elena and his disdain for Reinhardt. He knew that regardless of the outcome, the galaxy would be forever changed by the events unfolding before him.

And though he may have been a mere observer in this conflict, Victor knew that his role in shaping the future of the galaxy was far from over.

Chapter 3: Doubts

As Victor continued to watch the battle unfold below, a sense of unease crept over him once more, gnawing at the edges of his consciousness.

For years, he had devoted himself wholeheartedly to Alden's cause, believing it to be just and righteous.

But now, as he experienced the devastation and loss of life through war across the galaxy, doubts began to plague his mind.

He couldn't shake the feeling that perhaps there was another way, a path that didn't require so much bloodshed and suffering.
The image of Elena, fighting bravely against overwhelming odds, stirred something within him—a flicker of doubt that threatened to engulf his unwavering loyalty to Alden.

But just as doubt threatened to take root in his mind, the ground shook violently beneath him as Elena's mobile suit self-destructed in a blinding flash of light. The explosion rocked the battlefield, sending shockwaves rippling through the air and leaving devastation in its wake.

For a moment, Victor was frozen in shock, his mind reeling from the enormity of what had just occurred. The sight of Elena sacrificing herself for her cause struck a chord deep within him, stirring emotions he had long suppressed. As the dust began to settle and the echoes of the explosion faded into the distance, Victor found himself grappling with conflicting emotions.

On one hand, Victor felt a profound sense of admiration for Elena's sacrifice, her willingness to give her life for what she believed in. But on the other hand, he couldn't shake the feeling of doubt that lingered in the back of his mind.

Was all this death and destruction truly necessary?

Was there not a better way to achieve their goals without resorting to such extreme measures?

As he pondered these questions, Victor felt a pang of guilt gnawing at his conscience. He had sworn an oath to serve Alden without question, to obey his every command without hesitation. And yet, in this moment of doubt, he couldn't help but wonder if blind loyalty was truly the right path to follow.

But even as doubt clouded his mind, one thing remained clear—his love and loyalty to Alden. No matter the doubts that plagued him, Victor knew that he would stand by his fallen leader until the very end.

With a heavy heart, he turned his gaze back to the battlefield below, steeling himself for the challenges that lay ahead.

Whatever doubts he may have harbored, one thing was certain—his destiny was inexorably intertwined with that of Alden and the galactic empire. And come what may, Victor would do whatever it took to ensure their victory, even if it meant sacrificing everything he held dear.

RELIGIOUS SOLDIER

Chapter 1: Origins

Three centuries after the birth of Christ, amidst the shifting sands of time and the echoes of ancient civilizations, a clandestine cabal emerged from the shadows — the Religious Council.

Founded under the guise of piety and devotion, this enigmatic organization operated in the shadows, its true motives hidden from the world.

At first glance, the council appeared to be a beacon of light in a world shrouded in darkness. Its members are revered as wise and righteous leaders. They preached the virtues of faith and obedience.

But behind closed doors, a darker truth lurked — a truth known only to those initiated into the council's inner circle. For beneath their façade of benevolence lay a sinister agenda, driven by a lust for power and domination.

The council's origins traced back to a group of influential figures within the early Christian church, men and women who sought to wield their religious authority for their own gain. United by their thirst for control, they conspired in the shadows. Their ambitions fueled by a desire to shape the course of history to their will.

Under the guise of righteousness, the council manipulated kings and emperors, pulling the strings of power from behind the scenes. They amassed vast wealth and influence. Their reach extended far beyond the borders of any kingdom or empire. But as their influence grew, so too did their appetite for power. No longer content with mere manipulation, the council delved into darker pursuits, dabbling in forbidden arts and occult rituals in their quest for supremacy.

Their ranks swelled with the addition of ambitious and ruthless individuals drawn to the promise of untold riches and power beyond imagining.

Yet, amidst the shadows, whispers of the council's true nature began to spread — a whisper of fear and suspicion that grew louder with each passing day. Rumors of disappearances and dark sacrifices circulated among the populace, painting a grim picture of the council's deeds. But those who dared to speak out against the council soon found themselves silenced. Their voices snuffed out by unseen hands.

The council wielded its power ruthlessly, crushing dissent and quashing any who dared to oppose them.
And so, for three centuries, the Religious Council operated in the shadows. Its true nature is known only to those initiated into its dark rites. But as the world teetered on the brink of chaos, the council's grip on power began to falter, threatened by forces beyond their control.

In the depths of their secret chambers, the council's leaders plotted and schemed. Their desperation mounting as their carefully laid plans unraveled before their eyes. For in their arrogance, they had underestimated the resilience of those who stood against them—the brave few who dared to challenge their tyranny and fight for freedom.

And as the world stood on the precipice of a new era, the fate of the council hung in the balance. Its future is uncertain in the face of an uncertain world. For even the mightiest empires crumble, and the darkest shadows are eventually pierced by the light of truth.

Chapter 2: The Recruitment Technique

The fundamentals of the council brainwashing people to fulfill their darkest needs contributed to what a clandestine and methodical endeavor, shrouded in secrecy and manipulation consisted of.

In further detail, those techniques that involve recruitment share a method or approach used to accomplish a particular task or achieve a specific goal. It often involves a systematic and skillful application of principles, procedures, or practices to produce desired results in various fields such as art, science, sports, or craftsmanship.

They had centuries to develop techniques that range from simple procedures to complex processes and may involve a combination of knowledge, experience, and expertise.

Recruitment began with the selection of individuals deemed susceptible to the council's influence — those who were vulnerable, disillusioned, or easily swayed by promises of power and purpose. These individuals were carefully groomed and indoctrinated from a young age. Their minds molded to align with the council's twisted ideology.

The brainwashing techniques employed by the council were insidious and multifaceted, designed to break down the subject's sense of self and instill unwavering loyalty to the cause. Psychological manipulation, hypnosis, and sensory deprivation were just a few of the methods used to erode the individual's resistance and reshape their beliefs.

Under the guise of religious devotion and divine mandate, the council exploited their recruits' deepest fears and insecurities, convincing them that their actions were not only justified but ordained by a higher power. Through a combination of coercion, gaslighting, and psychological conditioning, the council ensured unwavering obedience from their followers.

Once fully indoctrinated, these brainwashed agents were deployed to carry out the council's nefarious agenda — assassinations, sabotage, espionage, and other unspeakable acts of violence and subterfuge.

Their minds warped by years of manipulation, they became willing instruments of the council's dark desires, devoid of empathy or remorse.

To maintain control over their operatives, the council employed a system of strict hierarchy and surveillance, ensuring that dissent was swiftly quashed and disobedience met with severe consequences. Those who dared to question or resist the council's authority were subjected to further brainwashing or disposed of without hesitation.

In this way, the council wielded their brainwashed agents as instruments of terror and oppression, manipulating them to carry out their bidding without question or hesitation.

Behind the facade of piety and righteousness, they lurked in the shadows, pulling the strings of their unwitting pawns to further their own twisted ambitions.

Chapter 3: Religious Relics

In the early days of humanity's expansion into the cosmos, the Religious Council, a clandestine organization rooted in ancient traditions, observed with keen interest as mankind reached out to the stars.

While the rest of humanity marveled at the wonders of the cosmos, the council saw an opportunity to advance their own agenda. As humanity's reach extended beyond the confines of their home planet, the council began to quietly infiltrate the highest echelons of power, using their influence to steer the course of human history.

They brokered secret deals with governments and corporations, exchanging their esoteric knowledge for access to advanced alien technology.

The council's agents scoured the galaxy for artifacts left behind by ancient civilizations, reverse-engineering their technology to suit their own purposes.

They experimented with alien alloys, harnessing their otherworldly properties to create powerful weapons and tools beyond the comprehension of ordinary humans.

With each new discovery, the council's power grew, their influence spreading like a virus throughout the galaxy. They established secret research facilities on distant planets and hidden moons where they conducted experiments in genetic engineering and artificial intelligence, pushing the boundaries of what was thought possible.

But as the council delved deeper into the mysteries of the cosmos, they attracted the attention of other, darker forces. Rival alien factions sought to challenge their dominance, launching covert operations and clandestine attacks in a bid to seize control of the alien technology for themselves.

The council fought back with ruthless efficiency, deploying their own agents and mercenaries to eliminate any threats to their power. They waged shadow wars across the galaxy, manipulating events from behind the scenes to maintain their stranglehold on humanity's destiny.

Despite their best efforts, however, the council could not prevent the inevitable. The discovery of alien artifacts sparked a gold rush among explorers and adventurers, leading to widespread chaos and conflict as rival factions fought over the spoils of the cosmos.

As humanity plunged headlong into a new era of uncertainty and upheaval, the council found themselves facing challenges unlike any they had ever encountered before. But even in the face of adversity, the council remained undaunted.

They had survived for centuries, weathering countless storms and emerging stronger than ever.

With the belief of God on the council's side, humanity stood on the brink of a new dawn, the council prepared to seize control of their destiny, their ambitions as boundless as the stars themselves.

Chapter 4: When Alden Was Recruited

Alden Vance stood amidst the chaos of the battlefield, his heart pounding in his chest as enemy forces closed in from all sides. Bullets whizzed through the air, explosions rocked the ground, and the acrid scent of smoke filled his nostrils.

Just as it seemed that all hope was lost, a hail of gunfire erupted from the shadows, cutting down Alden's would-be assailants with deadly precision.

In the blink of an eye, his mysterious savior emerged from the darkness clad in armor unlike anything Alden had ever seen. The armored figure moved with a grace and speed that defied belief, dispatching Alden's attackers with ruthless efficiency.

With each movement, it was as if time itself slowed. The figure's every action is calculated and deliberate. Alden could only watch in awe as the armored warrior fought with a skill and precision that bordered on the supernatural.

It was a sight to behold, a dance of death played out on the battlefield with deadly intent. As the last of Alden's assailants fell, the figure turned to face him. Its gaze pierced through the smoke and chaos.

There was a moment of silence between them, a shared understanding that transcended words.

Then, without a word, the figure extended a hand to Alden, offering him salvation in the midst of chaos. Alden hesitated for only a moment before grasping the offered hand, feeling a surge of gratitude wash over him.

"Who are you?" Alden asked, his voice barely above a whisper.

The figure regarded him with an intensity that sent shivers down Alden's spine.

"We are but God's soldiers," it replied cryptically, its voice echoing with an otherworldly resonance.

"Soldiers of a cause greater than ourselves."

Alden Vance stood at the precipice of destiny, his eyes scanning the battlefield strewn with the wreckage of war. A grim reminder of the chaos that engulfed the galaxy. It was in this moment of uncertainty that he felt a presence at his side.

The figure's armor shimmered with an otherworldly sheen. Its surface adorned with intricate patterns that seemed to dance in the faint light. At its side hung a weapon of alien design, its sleek form pulsating with energy.

"Commander Vance," the figure spoke, its voice echoing with an otherworldly resonance. "We have been watching you."

Alden turned to face the enigmatic stranger. His gaze locked onto the figure's piercing eyes.

"Who are you?" he demanded, his hand inching towards his laser pistol.

"We are but soldiers," the figure replied cryptically. Its voice tinged with an aura of mystery.

"Soldiers of a cause greater than ourselves."

Alden's curiosity was piqued, his eyes lingering on the alien weapon at the figure's side.

"What kind of soldiers?"

The figure stepped forward, its movements fluid and graceful.

"Soldiers who fight for the future of the galaxy," it answered. Its voice carried an otherworldly cadence.

"Soldiers who possess knowledge and technology beyond your wildest dreams."

Alden's mind raced with possibilities as he studied the alien weaponry before him. The allure of such power was undeniable. Its promise beckons him like a siren's call. But deep down, he knew that such power came with a price—a price he might not be willing to pay.

"What do you want from me?" Alden asked, his voice tinged with uncertainty.

"Your allegiance, Commander Vance," it replied.

"Your unwavering loyalty to our cause," its tone unwavering.

Alden hesitated, torn between duty and desire. The secrets to unyielding power were tempting, but he knew that accepting it would mean betraying everything he was. Needing someone's help.

"I need time to consider your offer".
Alden finally replied. His voice tinged with resolve.

The figure nodded. Its expression is unreadable behind the visor of its helmet.

"Take all the time you need, Commander Vance." it said.

"But remember, the fate of the galaxy hangs in the balance."

With that, the alien soldier turned and vanished into the shadows, leaving Alden alone with his thoughts.

As he watched the stars twinkling overhead, he knew that his decision would shape the course of history for generations to come.

It was at that moment Alden's path intersected with that of the enigmatic Religious Council.

Alden's ascent through the ranks of the military had caught the attention of the council who saw in him a potential pawn in their grand game of cosmic manipulation.

The council's agent approached Alden with an offer too tantalizing to refuse—a chance to wield power beyond his wildest dreams, to shape the fate of the galaxy itself.

Alden agreed to join forces with the council, setting in motion a chain of events that would alter the course of history forever. Under their guidance, he honed his skills as a leader and strategist, harnessing the secrets of the cosmos to further his own ambitions.

They spoke of ancient artifacts and forbidden knowledge, promising Alden the keys to unlocking his true potential.

ASSASSINS THAT RUN ON FAITH

Chapter 1: Why women are the perfect assassins.

In historical contexts, women were often considered prime candidates to be assassins due to a combination of factors, including their perceived beauty and their social standing within Christian societies.

Here's an exploration of those elements:

Perceived Vulnerability and Deception: Women were sometimes viewed as less threatening and more inconspicuous than men, making them ideal candidates for covert operations and assassination missions. Their perceived innocence and vulnerability could be used to their advantage, allowing them to gain access to targets and carry out missions without arousing suspicion.

Social Norms and Expectations: In many Christian societies, women were expected to adhere to traditional gender roles which often confined them to domestic duties and limited their opportunities for direct involvement in political or military affairs. This societal perception of women as passive and submissive could be exploited by clandestine organizations seeking to recruit assassins.

Access to Targets: Women, particularly those from privileged backgrounds or high social standings, often had access to influential figures, such as nobles, clergy, and royalty, through social circles, courtly engagements or domestic roles. Their proximity to potential targets made them valuable assets for espionage and assassination operations.

Use of Disguise: Women's attire, hairstyles, and mannerisms allowed them to blend seamlessly into various social settings, providing opportunities for infiltration and subterfuge. Disguised as servants, ladies-in-waiting, or members of the household staff, female assassins could move undetected within the inner circles of their targets, enabling them to carry out their missions with greater ease.

Manipulation of Social Norms: The prevailing social norms of the time often placed women in subordinate roles, which could be exploited by covert organizations to manipulate their actions and motivations. By appealing to their sense of duty, loyalty, or desire for autonomy, recruiters could enlist women as assassins, leveraging their skills and social status for the organization's benefit.

Emphasis on Subtlety and Subversion: Female assassins were often trained to employ methods that emphasized subtlety, cunning, and deception rather than brute force. Poisoning, seduction, and manipulation were common tactics used by female operatives to eliminate targets discreetly and avoid detection.

Overall, the combination of societal perceptions, social roles, and access to targets made women attractive candidates for assassination missions in Christian societies. Their ability to navigate social hierarchies, exploit gender stereotypes, and operate covertly allowed them to play crucial roles in clandestine operations throughout history.

Chapter 2: Duties

Women of the Religious Council operate under the guise of piety and devotion, the transition from nun to assassin might be surprisingly seamless.

Within the confines of their convent, these nuns undergo rigorous training in martial arts, stealth tactics, and the art of assassination under the pretense of spiritual discipline.

Under the guidance of a charismatic yet enigmatic leader known only as the High Abbess, the nuns are indoctrinated into a belief system that justifies violence as a means to uphold their interpretation of divine justice.

Through carefully crafted rituals and ceremonies, the sisterhood instills unwavering loyalty and obedience in its members, compelling them to carry out their deadly missions without question.

The convent itself serves as a clandestine training ground, equipped with state-of-the-art facilities hidden beneath its sacred halls of the Vatican on New Terra. Here, the nuns undergo physical conditioning, weapons training, and psychological manipulation designed to suppress empathy and foster ruthlessness.

Despite their outward appearance of piety and innocence, these nuns are trained killers, adept at blending into their surroundings and striking swiftly and silently when the need arises.

Disguised in their traditional habits, they move unnoticed through the shadows, executing their targets with cold precision before melting back into the sanctuary of their convent.

For those who dare to defy the sisterhood's teachings or question its authority, there is no mercy. Dissenters are swiftly dealt with either through covert assassination or public excommunication. Their fates serve as a chilling reminder of the consequences of disobedience.

In this dark and secretive world, the line between faith and fanaticism blurs, and the Sisterhood of Shadows wields its power with deadly efficiency, shaping the course of history through fear and manipulation.

Chapter 3: Amara's story

Amidst the shadows of tragedy in losing her parents to a terrorist organization trying to send a message to Alden's regime, Amara endured the cruelty inflicted upon her by those who should have offered love and protection within the state adoption system.

Raised in the confines of abuse, a household draped in the cloak of religiosity, she found herself subjected to mental and physical abuse for the slightest deviation from their strict beliefs.

Around the age of thirteen, she experienced the full weight of their disapproval, punished harshly for her perceived lack of faith and devotion. Their zealous fervor blinded them to her struggles. Their judgmental eyes cast her out as unworthy of their love and acceptance any time she rebelled.

Despite their claims of religious piety, their actions spoke volumes of their hypocrisy, leaving her to grapple with the pain of rejection and betrayal from the world.

Yet, in the depths of her despair, she turned to God, seeking solace and understanding in the arms of her faith.

By the time she reached the age of sixteen, she had found refuge within the sanctuary of the Catholic Church, where the gentle words of the priest offered her solace and comfort.

While confessing her sins and fears in the quiet solitude of the confessional. She poured out her heart and soul, laying bare the scars of her past for the healing touch of God's grace. With each whispered prayer, she felt the weight of her burdens lift, as though the darkness that had plagued her soul was slowly being washed away. Through her faith and the unconditional love of her spiritual family, she found the strength to confront the traumas of her upbringing, to embrace the light of God's love and forgiveness.

As she knelt before the altar, her heart overflowing with gratitude, she knew that she had finally found the peace and acceptance she had been searching for all along.

Chapter 4: The New Recruit

Amara's journey to the council began with a chance encounter, a fateful meeting that would forever alter the course of her life.

It was a quiet evening, much like any other, when she found herself kneeling in prayer before the altar of her parish church. Her heart is heavy with the weight of the world's burdens as if she alone is responsible for the evil in this galaxy.

As she poured out her soul in fervent supplication, she felt a presence beside her, a shadow cast by the flickering candlelight. Turning her gaze, she beheld the figure of her parish priest. His eyes were kind and understanding as they met hers.

"Child, I sense a great burden upon your heart," he said gently. His voice is a soothing balm to her troubled spirit.

"Tell me, what troubles you so deeply?"

With tears glistening in her eyes, Amara poured out her fears and doubts, confessing the struggles she had faced and the darkness that threatened to consume her.

She spoke of her longing for justice, for a world free from the tyranny of the wicked, her words echoing with a fervent belief in God's will to vanquish evil.

Rightened up by her passion and conviction, the priest listened intently, his heart heavy with empathy for the pain she had endured.

In that moment, he saw within her a spark of righteous indignation, a flame that burned brightly with the desire to right the wrongs of the world.

"It is clear to me, my child, that God has placed a calling upon your heart," the priest said solemnly, his gaze unwavering.

"But know this—sometimes, in order to confront evil, one must be willing to walk the path of darkness."

"Are you prepared to make that sacrifice?" he said in a sterner tone.

Amara's heart quickened with a mixture of fear and excitement. Her faith was bolstered by the priest's words of encouragement. She nodded solemnly. Her resolve was firm as she pledged herself to the service of God's will, no matter the cost.

And so it was that Amara found herself approached by the council, an enigmatic organization shrouded in secrecy and intrigue.

The Religious Council heard whispers of her devotion and her unwavering belief in God's divine justice and they saw within her the potential to be a powerful weapon in their ongoing war with anyone who stands in their way.

With the priest's blessing and her faith as her guide, Amara embarked on a journey into the unknown. Her path illuminated by the light of God's truth. And though she knew not what trials awaited her, she faced them with courage and determination, secure in the knowledge that she was fulfilling God's will to destroy the wicked and bring about a world of righteousness and peace.

Chapter 5: A Darkness Burns

In the quiet, candlelit halls of the Vatican, Amara knelt in prayer, her hands clasped tightly together as she whispered fervent words of devotion.

As a young novice, she had dedicated her life to serving God, surrendering herself completely to his will. But beneath her serene exterior lurked a darkness — a fire that burned with righteous fury. It was fueled by the injustices she had witnessed in the world beyond the convent walls.

For Amara was not just a nun; she was one of the Silent Sisters, a clandestine sisterhood of assassins trained to eliminate threats to the sanctity of their faith.

During her formative years from the ages of 16 to 21, Amara was secluded within the sacred walls of the Vatican, where she underwent rigorous training to fulfill her destined role as a Silent Sister.

Every aspect of her existence was meticulously shaped by the tenets of the holy scriptures, guiding her every step and action.

Under the watchful eyes of her mentors, Amara honed her skills in combat and espionage, mastering the art of wielding her blade with unparalleled precision and grace.

Her movements became a seamless dance of fluidity, akin to the gentle flow of water, yet harboring the lethal potency of tempered steel. But as she embarked on her one thousandth mission as a fully-fledged Silent Sister, doubts gnawed at the edges of her resolve.

The target of her assignment was a high-ranking official within the Ecclesiastical Guardians, accused of corruption and heresy against the gods.

Though Amara knew that her actions were sanctioned by the order, she could not shake the feeling of unease that gripped her heart.

Twenty years of searching for this fugitive, she finally found her prey through the labyrinthine streets of a small colony on Mars.

She spent most of her adult life studying this man, learning his history, his pain and his pleasure.

Somehow he was always one step ahead of her.

Until today.

Amara found herself confronted by memories of her past — a past filled with pain and suffering, a past that had driven her to embrace the path of the Silent Sisters.

But even as she grappled with her doubts, she knew that she could not falter in her mission.

Finally, she cornered her target in a secluded alleyway, her blade gleaming in the moonlight as she stepped forward to deliver the judgment of God.

But as she raised her weapon to strike, her resolve wavered. Her hand trembled with uncertainty. It was in that moment of hesitation that her target spoke, his voice calm and measured as he looked into her eyes with a gaze that pierced her soul.

"Do you truly believe that you are serving God?" he asked. His words echoing in the stillness of the night.

To her astonishment, his gaze showed no trace of fear as though he were certain that today was not the day he would meet his end. Amara faltered, her grip on her blade loosening as doubt clouded her mind.

"I...I do what I must to protect the sanctity of our faith," she replied, her voice barely above a whisper.

But her target shook his head, a sad smile playing at the corners of his lips. "The path you walk is not one of righteousness," he said. "It is a path of darkness and deceit, a path that leads only to despair."
In that moment, Amara saw the truth in his words—the truth that she had been too blind to see.

She quenched her blade harder. Her heart is heavy with the weight of her sins. As her target reached out to her with a hand of forgiveness, she knew that she could no longer continue down the path of the Silent Sisters.

She swiftly plunged the blade into his heart.

She held him up a moment longer, wanting to witness the departure of his soul from his eyes. "I'm sorry." she whispered. He smiled before his eyes dimmed.

With tears streaming down her face, she vowed to atone for her actions and seek redemption for the lives she had taken in the name of a faith that had betrayed her.

From that day onward, doubts about being a Silent Sister filled Amara's mind.

Chapter 6: The Beginning Of A New Path

Amara stood before the imposing figures of the council. Her heart is heavy with grief yet her resolve unyielding.

They had gathered in the hallowed chambers of the council to determine the next course of action in the wake of Alden's sacrifice. The echoes of his noble deed still reverberate through the galaxy.

"Amara," the council's leader intoned. His voice sounded like thunder in the solemn chamber.

"You have returned to us, bearing the weight of Alden Vance's demise upon your shoulders. Speak, and tell us what transpired in the final moments of his life."

Amara drew a steadying breath. Her gaze unwavering as she recounted the events that had led to Alden's ultimate sacrifice.

She spoke of their journey together, of the battles fought and the sacrifices made. Her words painted a vivid picture of their shared struggle against the relentless mechanoids.

"And in the end." she concluded. Her voice tinged with sorrow.

"Alden gave his life to save not only mine, but the galaxy itself. His loss will be felt by all who knew him."

The council members exchanged solemn glances. Their faces shrouded in contemplation.

For a long moment, silence reigned in the chamber, broken only by the soft rustle of robes and the faint hum of distant machinery.

Finally, the leader of the council spoke, his voice grave yet tinged with a hint of urgency. "Alden's sacrifice shall not be in vain," he declared. "But the galaxy remains in turmoil, and our enemies still lurk in the shadows waiting to seize upon our moment of weakness."

Amara nodded, understanding the gravity of the situation. Despite their victory with Alden, the council's enemies continued to pose a threat to the fragile peace they had fought so hard to preserve.

"We must remain vigilant," she said. Her voice was firm with determination.

"We cannot allow Alden's sacrifice to be in vain. We must honor his memory by continuing the fight against those who would seek to oppress and subjugate the innocent."

The council members nodded in agreement. Their expressions grim yet resolute. They knew that the road ahead would be fraught with peril, but they were prepared to face whatever challenges lay in their path.

And as they prepared to depart the chamber, Amara felt a flicker of hope ignite within her heart. Though Alden was gone, she believed his spirit lived on in their hearts, a beacon of light in the darkness, guiding them ever forward on their quest for justice and freedom.

After Amara left the chamber, the members of the council exchanged furtive glances, their voices lowered to whispers as they deliberated among themselves.

The weight of Amara's words hung heavy in the air. Their implications echoing through the hallowed halls of power.

"It seems our dear Amara has grown quite attached to Alden," one council member remarked. A sly smile playing at the corners of his lips.

"Perhaps his death could be... useful to us."

The others nodded in agreement. Their expressions shrouded in shadow.

They knew that Amara's emotions could be manipulated to serve their own ends. Her grief and guilt weaponized to further their agenda.

"It is a delicate matter," another council member mused, stroking his chin thoughtfully.

"But if we play our cards right, we could use Alden's death to bind her to us even more tightly than before."

The councilors nodded in silent accord. Their minds are already churning with schemes and stratagems. They were masters of manipulation, orchestrating events from the shadows to further their own ambitions.

"Let us proceed with caution," the leader of the council said firmly. His voice became a low rumble in the echoes of the dimly lit chamber.

"Amara may be a valuable asset, but she is also unpredictable. We must tread carefully if we are to keep her firmly under our control."

With that, the councilors dispersed. Their shadows melted into the darkness as they vanished into the labyrinthine corridors of power.

They knew that the game had only just begun, and that the stakes had never been higher.

For in the aftermath of Alden's death, Amara stood at a crossroads. Her loyalties are torn between duty and desire. And as the council plotted and schemed in the shadows, they knew that they held the key to shaping her destiny in the days to come.

ENDING WORDS

Thank you for reaching this milestone. I hope you've enjoyed this brief glimpse into the world of SINthetik Messiah.

This introductory book aimed to establish the dynamics of the galaxy and introduce key figures central to its structure. Stay tuned for further adventures!

With great love, Bug Gigabyte.

www.ingramcontent.com/pod-product-compliance
Lightning Source LLC
Chambersburg PA
CBHW061320120726
48001CB00002B/605